O'GRADY'S WELL

O'GRADY'S WELL

Heulwen Jones

ATHENA PRESS
LONDON

ISBN 1 84401 578 5

First Published 2005 by
ATHENA PRESS
Queen's House, 2 Holly Road
Twickenham TW1 4EG
United Kingdom

Printed for Athena Press

This book is dedicated to my immediate family, who have given me the support and encouragement to write this book.

CHAPTER ONE

It was a very damp, dismal day when the Delaney family arrived in Dublin airport, after a long trip from Boston, Massachusetts. *Typical Irish weather*, thought Danny who was the eldest of the three children. He had been dragged along by their mother and father on this holiday to Ireland. Danny's parents both had ancestors who were of Irish descent but Tom, Danny's father, had traced his back to the village of Kilnurrah, and so here he was on his quest to search for his great, great grandfather's history. Danny had wanted to go to summer camp in the mountains in Virginia that year with his classmates; but there was no way that he could change the minds of his mother and father – they were determined to embark on this quest and take their three children with them!

Danny's two siblings were Mary Ann and Ethan. Mary Ann was nine years old, Ethan was eleven and Danny was fifteen. He was at that age when tagging along with his younger brother and sister did not seem the 'cool' thing to do. They were still happy to play together and get amused by the most simple things, but Danny was a different personality altogether. He was more interested in discovering things and had a very vivid imagination. His imagination had got him into all sorts of trouble in the past, but he continued to be the 'joker' of the family and the one who always seemed to get into trouble. It was as if trouble sought him out wherever they went.

Danny was a good-looking boy and was sure to be a handsome young man in a few years. It was the charming way about him that had got him out of many a scrape in the past.

Mary Ann, on the other hand, was rather plain; she looked very much like her mother, Annie. They both had ginger hair but it always looked unkempt and both had lots of freckles and Mary Ann had very poor eyesight and had to wear very thick glasses. Annie had found it very difficult to lose any weight after having the children and, of course, her addiction to chocolate did not help, and so consequently she was very short and dumpy – not the petite college graduate that Tom had married. Danny resembled his father, who was a very good-looking man. He had dark, wavy hair and handsome facial features. He was over six feet tall and had a very good build. Many people wondered what on earth had attracted him to Annie, but in her younger day she had been quite pretty, and it was not until after the children had been born that her sweet tooth had taken a grip on her! They were like chalk and cheese: Annie had a very bad temper and Tom was always so calm and in control.

Then there was Ethan, who had brown hair just like his brother, but had to wear spectacles, which he hated. He was also at that age where he still had a lot of 'puppy fat', so he was very often bullied at school. He followed his brother around constantly, but after continually getting ignored he would eventually end up playing with his sister and they got on quite well.

The plane landed on the tarmac and it seemed like they had been on board for ever. The flight had taken eight hours from Boston. The captain's voice came over the tannoy and said, 'Good day, ladies and gentlemen, I hope you've enjoyed your flight with us. The weather in Dublin today is very unsettled and the temperature is ten degrees Celsius. May I take this opportunity to thank you for flying with Air Ireland and hope you have a safe journey to your final destination.'

The Delaney's destination was another four hours away by car, which Tom had arranged to hire at the airport.

'Come along, stop daydreaming,' said Annie to the children. 'You'll all have to start looking after your own luggage – I'm fed up of having to take care of everything,' as she tugged at a bag from the overhead locker. Tom looked at the children in a knowing way as if to say, 'Don't worry – I'll take care of things.' The whole family got off the plane and after collecting their luggage and going through passport control Tom headed off for the car hire company booth in the foyer of the terminal building.

The family passed a few shops in the airport building and as Danny passed by he noticed a few toy leprechauns. They seemed to come in all sorts of items: stuffed ones, keyrings, hats – there was no end to what a leprechaun could be made into here in Ireland! Danny turned to his mother and said, 'Do you believe in leprechauns, Mom?'

Annie curtly replied, 'Don't be crazy – and don't let that imagination of yours get you into trouble on this vacation.' That reply dampened any dim hope that Danny might get some enjoyment out of this holiday – he really wasn't interested in tracing his ancestry but finding a leprechaun – well, that was another story...

Tom beckoned to the family to join him at the other end of the building – he'd got the car and yet another long journey was due to begin – this time on the road in the pouring rain.

They all piled into the car and packed the luggage in the back, which didn't leave a lot of room for movement. Danny was really tired; if he could just go to sleep for the four-hour journey then that would be great, he could block out the boredom and the incessant chattering of his younger brother and sister. He also knew that before too long there would be some 'entertainment' in the form of his mother being tetchy towards his poor father. Oh no, he couldn't stand this!

They drove out of the airport and slowly Danny managed to drift off…

Eventually they arrived at their destination, a place called Kilnurrah. The sun had come out somewhere between Dublin and Kilnurrah and it looked an 'OK' place, Danny thought. Everywhere was very green; green trees, green grass – greener than Danny had ever seen. Kilnurrah was a small village on the west coast this was where their ancestors had apparently journeyed from when they emigrated to America in the 1800s.

Kilnurrah was a busy, one street village, and that was it. It was built in a circle and the single road went around the town so it was impossible to get lost as there were no roads or streets off anywhere. The village looked like something out of a faerietale – quaint, small houses painted white with red or green doors. There were a few shops, a pub and a church, but that was all. However, in the distance just outside the village, Danny could see that there was a wooded area. Although it wasn't very big, he could see that it got really dark as you looked through the trees. Danny immediately felt that the wood looked a sad place – if it were possible for a wood to be sad. He couldn't quite understand why he had this feeling, but nevertheless it was there and it felt strange. Even though the sun was out, there didn't seem to be any sunlight getting through the leaves to the ground. Surrounding the wood was a field of the greenest grass he'd ever seen, with a red gate in the wall surrounding the field bearing message KEEP OUT in both English and Gaelic. This of course was translated in Danny's mind as MUST HAVE A LOOK.

Tom drove up alongside a small cottage that was painted all in white except for the paintwork around the windows and doors, which was bright green. The name above the door read O'GRADY'S WELL. Danny felt as though he had entered a 'green' world with very little else in terms of colour surrounding him. The cottage had been rented by the family for the two-week vacation and it was intended to be a good base for them to carry out their investigations into their family tree.

They all piled out of the car feeling very tired and cranky. Annie, being her usual self, said, 'I'm too tired to get dinner; you'll all have to fend for yourselves. I'm off for a sleep and don't anyone disturb me.' Tom had noticed that there was a small coffee shop in the village so he said, 'Right kids, we'll freshen up and then we'll go to the coffee shop to get some food.'

Ethan piped up, 'But I want a burger.'

Tom looked at him in a don't-hassle-me-now kind of way and said, 'We left the burgers in the States. You're going to eat food like your ancestors ate for these two weeks – good wholesome cooking.'

The inside of the cottage was small but adequate. There was a small kitchen, lounge and bathroom downstairs and upstairs were three bedrooms, so, much to Danny's delight, he had a room with a double bed all to himself. Ethan and Mary Ann were to share the twin room and his parents were in the other double. Danny went straight to his room and locked the door as if to make a statement to the rest of the family right from the start. That was his instruction like the one on the gate which read KEEP OUT. Danny sat on the chair that was next to the window and looked out at the view; his room looked directly out onto the wood that he had seen earlier. He sat with his elbows on the windowsill and his hands under his chin, just looking and thinking and said to himself, *I'm sure there's an adventure waiting to happen in there.*

A loud knock on his bedroom door brought Danny back from the brink of that adventure – at least for the time being. It was his father and the others, standing there with a look that said 'come on, we're starving!'

'Are you coming with us to the coffee shop, Dan?' Tom said.

Danny said, 'Yes, but can I go exploring afterwards?'

'It'll be getting dark in about an hour, maybe tomorrow.'

Danny's heart sank, it looked light enough to him but he could see the sun going down in the distance behind the wood, and that made it look even more mysterious. Maybe his father was right; after all, they were here for two whole weeks. Danny wasn't sure whether that was something he should be excited about or not.

The three children and their father left the cottage and walked down the cobbled street to the coffee shop. Danny noticed that there were no electric street lights, only old-looking lamps stuck on posts every few hundred yards. 'What happens when it gets dark here, Pop?' Danny asked his father.

'These are gas lamps, son, and someone will probably come around before it gets dark to light them,' Tom answered.

Oh, this place is really in the past – no burgers and no electric light! Danny thought. This would probably mean no

TV in the cottage and everyone would have to be in bed by the time it got dark. Oh this holiday was really beginning to sound fun!

The family eventually arrived at the coffee shop. The name above the door read OONAGH'S COFFEE COTTAGE. The shop was painted white with green paintwork around the windows and doors. There were window boxes on each of the window sills full of brightly coloured flowers, which made the outside of the building look very quaint, and the smell of freshly brewed coffee and newly baked bread made the inside of the coffee shop smell very inviting indeed – especially since they hadn't eaten for about eight hours. The last meal they'd had was on the plane and Danny recalled it as being very much like cardboard and fries. The menu had said chicken and chips (fries), but you'd have to have a very good imagination to think that the object served with the fries had ever been a chicken! Dessert had been some kind of chocolate mousse but had actually looked and tasted like a soggy mess with bits of what was described as chocolate – rather than ask too many questions Danny was happy to accept the description as the truth. So by now anything on the menu in this joint would have seemed like nectar from the gods.

Tom and the children sat at a table near the window. There was a candle in the middle of the table and the table cloth and the cutlery were spotlessly clean. The knives and forks glistened in the shimmering candlelight. Over the other side of the room there was a log fire – it was beginning to get cold now so it was welcoming to feel the heat and hear the crackling of the logs in the fireplace. It was an inglenook fireplace with seats either side of the fire. Danny couldn't help staring at the fire dancing in the hearth, it were as if he were mesmerised. At home they had electric heating and none of the children had really seen a fire in a fireplace before. The nearest Danny had ever got to a fire like this was when he went camping, but this fire was different somehow – it seemed to come alive.

The next thing Danny felt was a nudge in the ribs from his sister. 'Danny, Dad's speaking to you!' she hissed.

Unbeknown to Danny, his father had been studying the menu with his brother and sister and they had all chosen what they wanted and now it was Danny's turn. Danny snapped himself out of what he thought was another daydream. The trip had been a long one and maybe now it was beginning to catch up with him.

Danny decided that he'd also try the Irish stew with soda bread. Tom looked around to see if he could find a waitress. When they had come into the coffee shop he'd been so eager to find a menu that he hadn't really noticed that there weren't any other people there and no waiter or waitress either. Tom got up and walked over to a small wooden counter with a small bell on it and a sign attached to the bell saying PLEASE RING FOR SERVICE. Tom did this and then he heard some movement down a corridor that led off from the counter.

He heard tiny footsteps and a lot of chattering and whispering and then appeared the shortest waitress he'd ever seen. She was an old lady about three feet tall with spectacles perched on the end of her nose. She had a scarf tied around her head and knotted firmly underneath her chin. She was dressed in a long skirt with an apron as white as snow and a blouse to match.

Tom stepped back – he didn't know what he had expected exactly, but this certainly wasn't it! The old lady acted in a very peculiar manner and said in a broad southern Irish accent, 'Oh I'm terribly sorry sir, I've been feeding the chickens out the back and I didn't know anyone was in the shop – now, what can I get you and your fine family?'

Danny immediately felt that there was something strange about this little old lady. He couldn't help but interpret 'I've been feeding the chickens' to mean 'I've been feeding the chickens *to* something'! The elderly waitress gave the impression that she hadn't been expecting them, but Danny felt that she knew all along that they would be coming to *that* coffee shop *that* night.

Tom said, in a startled voice, 'We'll all have the Irish Stew with some soda bread and four coffees please.'

The old lady answered, 'Oh, to be sure that's a good choice, are you staying locally?'

'Yes, we're staying at the O'Grady place just up the road,' Tom answered.

She immediately looked at Danny and gave him the strangest stare.

By this time Tom had got over the shock of seeing such an unusual hostess and was beginning to feel more relaxed in her company. The children, on the other hand, were just sat at the table looking at the old lady, totally dumbstruck with mouths open as if they couldn't believe their eyes. She certainly was not the usual gum-chewing, spotty youth dressed in a tacky uniform that they were sometimes used to in fast food restaurants back home.

Tom said to the old lady, 'Do you have some Irish folk music that we could listen to on the sound system while we are waiting?'

The old lady looked bemused. 'Sound System'? What on earth did they mean?

Then Tom realised what a stupid request he'd made – no electricity = no sound system. He became really embarrassed and said, 'Oh, I'm sorry, it's just we left the States less than twenty-four hours ago and it takes a bit of adjusting to – no electricity, I mean.'

The old lady smiled but with a sly look in her eyes and exposed a set of really bad teeth. This turned Danny off his Irish stew even before he got it. *If she's cooked it – uggh!* he thought,

Danny and the other children had been brought up by Annie to be scrupulously clean and that meant paying attention to personal hygiene, even brushing teeth after every meal, so he noticed things like bad teeth. Strange, though, because everything else about her and the coffee shop seemed so clean and in order. Anyway, she scuttled away down the passage to what everyone hoped was the kitchen.

Danny looked out of the window – his father was right; it was getting dark outside so after the meal the only place left to go would be the cottage and probably then to bed. He fully expected his mother to sleep all the time they were out and all through the night. She was a very heavy sleeper and needed at least ten hours' sleep a night, otherwise she was in a terrible mood the following day. The children always knew when their mother hadn't had much sleep – nothing, absolutely nothing they said or did was right. She'd be really tetchy; however, there was an up side: if there was a spare box of chocolates floating around the house that usually pacified her for an hour or so. *No wonder she's so over-weight*, Danny thought…

Outside, the sky was turning a mysterious navy blue colour. The only light came from the candles on the five tables in the little coffee shop, and of course the log fire which by now was raging in the fireplace. The reflection of the candlelight and the light from the fire seemed to be dancing around the room across the walls and the ceiling. The fire was spitting cinders onto the flagstone floor and up into the chimney. There was a dim light coming from the passage the old lady had disappeared down, but that was it.

Danny hoped that someone would be lighting the street lights pretty soon, otherwise it would be a wobbly walk back to the cottage – they didn't know the road very well and cobbles were not that easy to walk on, even in daylight. This was especially true for Mary Ann, who had insisted on buying a new pair of shoes for the trip and, in accordance with the fashion sense of her peers, they had big thick high heels; totally impossible for her to walk in at her age and even more impossible on cobbles! She would no doubt return to her trainers within the next few days, fashion having lost the battle against comfort.

Eventually the family could hear the noise of tiny foot-steps in the passage and the smell of something delicious coming with them. The old lady reappeared carrying a tray with four bowls of steaming stew and a plate of soda bread. She balanced the tray on the end of the table and handed each of them a bowl then put the bread at the side. 'Well, here we are then, I'm sure you'll enjoy. Just leave the money on the counter when you leave – good night sleep tight,' she said.

Tom and the children were by this time so hungry that they didn't pay much attention to how their waitress looked or what she said; they just scoffed the food. It wasn't until after they had finished that Tom thought how trusting she was to allow perfect strangers to just leave the money on the counter.

Anyway, after Danny finished his stew he noticed that as if by magic, the lights had all come on outside in the street – he hadn't noticed anyone putting them on, but he thought maybe that was because he had been too busy eating; after all, he was starving.

The family got up from the table, the chairs making a scraping noise as they were drawn across the stone floor. Tom thought that this din would bring the old lady back – but no sign. He did what she said and left the money on the counter. They started walking towards the door and Tom and the two youngest were chatting about what they were going to do the next day, when Danny suddenly noticed something strange over by the fireplace. He had been mesmerised by the fire since the moment he came in, and as he took a last glance, as if to say goodbye, he saw the strangest thing…

CHAPTER TWO

Danny could see the old lady, but this time she wasn't dressed in her long skirt and apron, she was wearing a green dress with what looked like a piece of rope tied around the middle and on her head, instead of the scarf, she wore a pointed hat that exposed what the scarf had been hiding – her ears. These were the longest you'd ever seen. They were pointed but the point spiralled up into a corkscrew shape and the top of the spiral reached almost as high as the point of her hat. She was smoking a clay pipe and between puffs was chuckling mischievously and looking straight at Danny with piercing eyes. Her hair was stuffed up into the hat and the skin on her face matched her teeth – it was really bad. The teeth were black, as before, but the skin was now pock-marked and he could see big boils all over her cheeks and one massive one at the end of her nose, which had grown to be much longer than before. Danny noticed that her hands around the clay pipe were bony and wrinkled.

Then all at once she disappeared. Danny shouted to his father, who was by this time outside on the pavement with the other children. 'Dad, Dad! I've just seen the most horrible thing!'

'Danny, what are you talking about? Don't start your nonsense on this holiday please – I don't want your mother getting upset – let's just try to enjoy these two weeks, please Danny,' Tom replied, the warning implicit in his voice.

Danny knew there was no point in continuing with this conversation. Who would believe him anyway – he could hardly believe himself! Was this the tiredness creeping up on him and playing tricks on his imagination? He didn't think so. The old lady had definitely seemed weird when she'd served them, but was his imagination just looking for something to spice up this holiday?

Tearing himself away, Danny joined his family and closed the door to the coffee shop, and as soon as he did this all the candles in the shop went out immediately. Strange…

Tom walked with his family up the cobbled street towards the cottage; the lamplight certainly helped them to dodge the more uneven parts of the cobbles. To everyone's amazement Annie must have woken up, because they could see candlelight in the windows. They knew she'd be unhappy about the fact that there was no TV because she was a soap opera addict and was firmly under the impression that they would have a satellite TV in the cottage so she could keep up with the episodes she'd miss in the US. They walked up to the door in trepidation and sure enough there were candles everywhere – but no Annie. Tom went upstairs to check the bedroom and there she was: blissfully sleeping, unaware of anything.

Tom thought maybe there was a house-sitter who came to check that everything was OK for the new arrivals and hadn't wanted to disturb Annie, and they had lit the candles. Maybe candles lit themselves in this place just like the ones on the roadside had suddenly come alive on their own? Anyhow, it was too late to try to rationalise anything; they were all tired and needed to sleep. Tomorrow was another day.

Tom made sure that Mary Ann and Ethan were tucked up in their beds and Danny said goodnight to his father and went to his room. Danny walked over to the window to close the curtains and, just as he was drawing them together, he noticed there was a dim light out in the wood where earlier there had been complete darkness – not even the sunlight had penetrated that part. Danny opened his window to make sure that it wasn't a reflection on the glass from the candle inside his room. This just confirmed what his eyes were telling him; there *was* a light there and in the distance he could hear Irish music. He was sure it was coming from the wood. *That's strange*, thought Danny, *there's no electricity here to have records played, so someone must be* playing *this music*. It was very sad music, with the very haunting sound of the Irish pipes.

Danny closed his window and his curtains and very thoughtfully got into bed – what was out there? Maybe it was a farmhouse or something? Why the big 'keep out' sign? He would have to investigate, but it would be difficult to get time away from his family without them noticing he was gone. Both his mother and father were determined that he was going to learn about his ancestors on this trip, and he had already been told he wasn't going to be allowed to wander and get into trouble. This was a family holiday and that meant the family would be spending it together.

The following morning Danny was woken by the sun streaming through the gap in his curtains. It was nine o'clock and he couldn't hear anyone else moving about yet; the jet lag had probably kicked in. It was pointless going downstairs for any breakfast because there wasn't any food, but he was hungry again and was desperate for a cup of coffee. He got out of bed and slowly staggered to the window to open the curtains. He was reminded of the strange events of the night before and looked cautiously at the wood just across the field.

Now, from outside he could hear the sounds of people going about their daily lives. Everything sounded so normal; the postman was ringing the bell on his bike to get a dog out of his way on the road; the milkman was whistling and clanking bottles together as he delivered them; the bakery up the road must have been doing their morning bake because the smell of fresh bread was creeping into Danny's room. People were greeting each other in a normal, friendly way, and what Danny noticed was that none of these people were tiny like the old lady last night in the coffee shop; they were all 'normal' size.

Bored, Danny decided to check if the rest of his family were awake yet. He tip-toed quietly to his brother and sister's room first and then to his parents' room; they were still fast asleep, so he decided to have a walk around the town himself and maybe get some breakfast somewhere, although he was determined that he wasn't going back to the coffee shop – at least not on his own.

As Danny stepped out of the cottage he thought it was going to be a lovely day, the weather was very sunny and it would probably get quite warm later. He retraced his steps from the night before and passed the coffee shop. He was determined he wasn't going to even look in there, but his curiosity got the better of him. When he peeked through the window he saw a totally different sight from the one that had greeted him the night before. There was a young girl about his age serving at the tables – she was, he thought, absolutely gorgeous. She had long, shiny blonde hair, and looked perfect in every way. As Danny was looking at her she glanced up and looked at him with the most beautiful blue eyes. She smiled shyly and hurried away down the corridor the old woman had gone down the night before. Danny thought, *Well, maybe this isn't such a bad place after all*, and his memories of the night before and determination to explore the wood seemed to fade a little. There were other interesting possibilities emerging now!

Danny was drawn into the coffee shop, even though he'd promised himself that he wouldn't go there. He thought he'd just get a coffee and try to get a conversation going with this mysterious female. He walked over to the table where he'd sat with his family the night before and picked up the menu. No sooner had he done this than the girl reappeared and walked over to his table. She spoke with the softest Irish accent and said, 'Good morning to you, and what can I get you this morning?'

Danny just looked up at the beautiful blue eyes smiling down at him and said nothing; it was as if he were under a spell of some kind. The girl asked him again, 'Can I get you something to eat or drink maybe?'

Danny awoke from the trance that he was in and said, in a flustered way, 'Yes, yes – I'd like a cup of coffee please, and maybe a bagel with cream cheese and grape jelly.'

The girl said, 'I'm sorry, but we don't do bagels – would you like some toast maybe?'

Danny replied, 'Yes, that's fine – sorry, I'm finding it hard to adjust to being outside the US, it's my first time in Europe. What's your name?'

'Brianna,' the girl replied.

'I'm Danny – pleased to meet you.' Danny held out his hand to shake hers but she looked around nervously and quickly stepped away, saying, 'I'll get your breakfast.'

The weather was beginning to change outside – it was now overcast and the sun had definitely disappeared. Danny felt a little disappointed that Brianna hadn't wanted to shake his hand he felt that was a definite 'leave me alone' statement. But like most fifteen-year-old boys he got over the rejection very quickly and thought, *Oh well, plenty more fish in the sea.*

About ten minutes later Brianna reappeared with the

breakfast. She was still quite pleasant but also distant in her manner. Danny thanked her for the food and as she turned to walk away, Danny thought he'd have another go at a conversation. He shouted, 'Excuse me, do you have any jam or marmalade?'

She turned around and said, 'I'll get you some.'

When she returned Danny said, 'I was here last night with my father and younger brother and sister – we had Irish stew – very good it was too. Do you work in the evenings?'

Brianna just looked at him in a puzzled kind of way and replied, 'We don't open in the evenings – we close at four o'clock every day.'

Danny said, 'You must be mistaken – we were here at eight o'clock last night until around nine.'

Brianna just shook her head and a worried expression crossed her face and she hurried off.

Danny was beginning to lose patience with his new found acquaintance; first of all she wouldn't shake his hand and now she was calling him a liar. *Strange girls over here*, he thought to himself.

Half way through his coffee and toast Danny remembered what he'd seen as he was leaving the coffee shop the previous night and thought maybe he wasn't wrong about it, maybe he didn't imagine it. He decided that there was definitely something really strange about this place, but he wouldn't mention it to his father or the others because he knew they'd just accuse him of being his usual, over-imaginative self. Maybe he should make some enquiries of his own and do a bit more exploring around this little village...

He left the money for his breakfast on the counter as his father had done the night before and walked back towards the cottage. He could feel spots of rain on his face and thought, *Here we go, another day in sunny Ireland*. His earlier positive thoughts about the weather were set to be well and truly dashed. When he got back to the cottage his parents and his brother and sister were awake and were getting ready to go to the grocer's to get some food.

'Where have you been, Danny?' Tom asked.

'I was a bit hungry so I thought I'd go to the coffee shop for some breakfast,' Danny replied.

'Was that old woman there?'

'Er, no Dad, they must work shifts there – there was a young girl there this morning,' Danny replied hesitantly.

Tom seemed happy with this explanation and didn't question Danny further. 'We're off to go and get some food from the grocer's,' he said. 'Do you want to come?'

Danny gave his father a look that said 'do you think I'm stupid?' and Tom said, 'Well, I guess it's not really your scene – we'll see you later,' and they all went off to the grocer's leaving Danny alone in the cottage.

Danny thought to himself, *This'll be my chance to go up to the gate and maybe venture into the wood to see what's there*. He knew they'd be gone for a while as his mother was a shopaholic and although there weren't many shops in the village, he knew she'd make the absolute utmost of whatever there was.

Danny went to the door hesitantly, just to make sure that they'd gone and then started on his way down the lane that led from the village towards the gate. He got to the red gate and just as he put his hand on the latch to open it a strange feeling shot up his arm. He pulled his hand away quickly. There was definitely something strange here. He needed to find out more and he had a strong feeling that he knew who could tell him – Brianna.

Although he had 'temporarily' fallen in love with Brianna over his cup of coffee and two pieces of toast, Danny had the feeling that there was more to this girl than met the eye. Something just didn't add up, and certainly what she had said about the coffee shop didn't make any sense.

Danny started walking back to the village and decided that he'd try to find the rest of his family. He passed the O'Grady cottage and re-read the name over the door: O'GRADY'S WELL. *Well?* he thought, *where's the well?' Maybe there was a story behind this name...*

He continued in the direction he thought would take him to the grocer's where his family had headed about half an hour earlier. He passed a few more cottages; people who were chatting to their neighbours just stared at him as he walked by. He saw the postman again, getting mail out of the post box, and the milkman was delivering cream to the bakery. All these people seemed to be 'normal' but there was something that he couldn't quite put his finger on.

As Danny walked into the grocer's shop he saw his long suffering father and siblings waiting for Annie. She seemed to be looking at every item on the shelves of this shop. Tom was carrying a basket which was already full to overflowing, but still she continued to pack things in. Danny noticed four boxes of chocolates piled on the top. He just shook his head and looked at his father, who knew what his son was thinking and rolled his eyes to the ceiling as if to say 'What can I do?'

As Danny walked over, his father said out loud, 'Hi Dan, where have you been?'

'Oh, I just went for a walk.'

'What do you think of the village?' Tom asked. 'We're going over to the church later to try to find out some information from the church records about our ancestors.'

Danny looked totally disinterested and grunted, 'Oh yeah?'

'Try to look a bit more interested, Dan, they were your great, great, great grandparents and their families you know –

don't you want to find out what they were like and what they got up to?'

Danny couldn't contain himself any longer he had to say what he felt. 'Well *no*, actually I *don't* care.'

By now Annie had finished her mammoth shop and over-heard what Danny had said. Even though she'd had a full ten hours sleep the night before she still didn't allow the children to be disrespectful to either her or their father and she hit him across his shoulders with a very large loaf of bread. 'Apologise to your father,' she snarled.

Danny said sorry but knew that this meant he would be watched even more and expected to partake in the 'walking around the cemetery, looking for info' activities with enthusiasm.

Even though Brianna was as distant from Danny as Boston was from Dublin, he still felt he had to find a way to approach her again, even if it were only to break up the boredom and have someone else to talk to of his own age for the next two weeks.

The family walked back to the cottage and on the way it suddenly dawned on Danny what was strange about everyone in the village: they all wore some kind of headgear. The postman had a hat; the milkman had a flat cap; the baker had a net hat; even the grocer had a woolly hat on and practically all the women had scarves on and they all had their ears covered. The only one that didn't wear anything on her head was Brianna. Could this have something to do with the horrible ears that he'd seen on the old woman in the coffee shop the night before?

When they got back to the cottage Annie set about making brunch for everyone and during the meal they chatted about what they were going to do that afternoon. Tom had decided to walk along to the church and see if there was anyone there who could give him some information. Annie and the children went to have a look at the old part of the cemetery to try to find out where their ancestors were buried. Danny really couldn't see what all this was going to get them but because of the clout he got in the grocer's he thought he'd best go along with things – at least for the time being.

The whole family set out at about two o'clock to go to the church. When they arrived Tom knocked on the door of a small house. The door was opened by a tubby little man. He was only about five feet tall, but he was dressed like a monk and had a brown cassock on with the hood up over his head. Danny couldn't help but think, *Well surprise, surprise he's hiding his ears as well!* The cassock was tied around his waist with a rope. He had piercing eyes like the old woman and seemed to stare at Danny the whole time Tom was talking to him.

Tom explained that they had come to try to locate some information and maybe the graves of their ancestors who they understood had lived and died in Kilnurrah a long time ago. The little man took Tom and Annie into the church and showed them some old census books listing people who had lived in the village, and so Tom set about looking through them. The strange little man then took Annie outside and pointed to an area in the cemetery where he thought it would be likely that Tom's great, great grandparents were buried. The younger children seemed to get a great sense of fun running in and out of the gravestones and playing a macabre game of hide and seek.

The 'old' part of the cemetery was almost right next to the wall that surrounded the green field. It was very easy to see the wood from here and Danny stood close to the wall and stared over at the mysterious wood. It was very frustrating for him to be so close and yet so far. He daren't try to sneak off just yet – his mother was watching his every move. Sooner than expected, though, his chance came.

The cemetery was very overgrown and the ground was boggy and uneven. Danny heard a terrible scream and looked around just in time to see his mother disappear down a hole that had been hidden by some moss, which had grown over some bushes which had looked like solid ground from above.

Annie screamed and yelled like something terrible was chasing after her. Tom came running out of the church to help, and the younger children ran to try to help their mother. Danny, still feeling the pain from his whack across the shoulder, had no sympathy whatsoever and took advantage of the distraction. He headed off in the opposite direction to make an unnoticed and hasty exit in the midst of all the commotion.

Danny was almost at the gate of the churchyard when he heard a rustling in the bushes, which were up against the wall. He looked towards where the noise was coming from, thinking it was a bird or a small animal that had got caught, but then to his fright he saw an odd-looking little man dressed in the strangest clothes. The little man looked really nervous and flustered and beckoned Danny over. Danny didn't know what to do and looked around to see if anyone else was about before walking slowly towards him.

Danny had a better view of this man now – he was about two feet six inches tall, had long, ginger hair and a long ginger beard that trailed on the floor. His face was as red as a berry, with droplets of perspiration dripping down his forehead onto his eyebrows, which were so long they curled upwards, above the bluest eyes Danny had ever seen. His clothes were patches of material that had been sewn together in no particular fashion to make a jacket and trousers. The bottoms of the trousers were cut very unevenly and on his feet he wore an old looking pair of leather boots. The little man seemed very agitated, and Danny wasn't sure who was the most frightened, him or the little man.

When Danny got up closer the little man said in a hurried, lilting Irish accent, 'Listen, there's not much time, I've got to tell you something and you've got to listen—' But then just at the most crucial point there was a shout from Tom, 'Danny, *Danny!* Where are you? I need your help – your mother's broken her leg.'

With that the little man vanished into thin air leaving Danny feeling really frustrated and angry at Tom's timing. He ran over to his father who was trying to hold his mother up – she had her arm around his neck and it was difficult to work out which, of the two of them, had the look of most pain on their face.

Tom spluttered, 'I'm going to have to take her to the hospital – can you look after yourself for a couple of hours? By the time an ambulance gets here we could be half way to the hospital. It'll be quicker this way. I'll get back as soon as I can.'

Danny didn't hesitate to say 'OK', and was just about to say 'Don't rush', but he held these words back realising they might arouse suspicion. This was the 'break' he'd been waiting for. He didn't want to be heartless towards his mother but she could be an old dragon sometimes, and after all she should have looked where she was going in such an old and disused graveyard.

Tom got the car and piled Annie into the back seat so she could stretch her leg out. Mary Ann insisted on sitting in the back with her mother to play nurse and Ethan sat in the front. They didn't want to stay with Danny. Ethan had somehow imagined that his father was going to be driving as fast as ambulances did and he wasn't going to miss that for anything. Danny watched them drive off into the distance. The hospital was about a two-hour drive away, so he really didn't have any idea when he'd next see his family again.

Now that he had his freedom at last, Danny thought he'd go to check out the coffee shop again, but sure enough it was shut just like Brianna had said; there was a sign on the door saying it closed at four o'clock. It was now six and he had no idea where Brianna lived so he couldn't even just hang around in her area on the off chance of bumping into her.

Disheartened, Danny went back to the bush in the church-yard where he'd seen the little man but there was no one there. He went to the cottage and sat in his bedroom looking out over the fields to the wood but nothing seemed to be happening there either.

Danny searched for his books in his luggage and read for about an hour and then his mobile phone rang. It was Tom telling him that his mother would have to stay at the hospital for a couple of days. She'd had a very bad fracture and Tom and the children would have to find a bed and breakfast near the hospital to be close to her. 'Are you sure you'll be OK there for a few days? There's plenty of food in the cupboard, or do you want me to come to get you?' Tom asked.

'No, don't come back all this way, I'll be fine, I'll hire a fishing rod and do some fishing in the river and I'll do some reading – I've brought plenty of books. I'll keep in touch by phone. Take care, Dad, and give my love to Mom. Bye,' Danny replied, unable to keep the excitement from his voice. He was now free – for a few days at least – to find out what exactly was going on in this place. He snuggled up under the covers and fell asleep, with a wide grin on his face.

CHAPTER THREE

Danny woke the following morning and decided not to make breakfast for himself; after all there would be the washing up to do and he wasn't having any of that. Anyway, he had an ulterior motive for 'dining out', he wanted to see Brianna again. He got dressed and headed out, down the street, towards the coffee shop. Sure enough there she was, looking as beautiful as the first time he saw her. He checked his reflection in the window to make sure there wasn't a hair out of place, walked into the shop and sat at what was becoming his 'regular' table.

Danny studied the menu again, trying to look intellectual, and tried to remember not to order anything that wasn't on the menu this time!

After about five minutes Brianna walked over to his table. 'How are you today?' she said.

'I'm fine,' replied Danny, and he just grabbed the moment. 'It's Sunday tomorrow – do you have a day off on a Sunday?'

'Yes, I do,' replied Brianna.

'Would you like to show me the area on your day off? My mother has had to go to the hospital – she had an accident yesterday and my family have to stay close by so I'll be on my own for a few days.'

'Oh, that's too bad,' said Brianna.

Just as Danny thought Brianna was going to agree to spend the day with him, a voice called her from down the corridor. 'I'll have to go,' she said nervously.

'But what about my breakfast?' asked Danny.

'I'll be back in a short while,' replied Brianna.

But even though Danny waited for about half an hour there was still no sign of Brianna; it was as if she'd disappeared. From down the corridor came an older looking man. A miserable looking specimen, he shuffled as he walked, dragging his feet on the stone floor. He was dressed very untidily. He was unshaven, had bad teeth and his hair looked as if it had not seen a comb in years. He asked Danny what he wanted for breakfast, and at the same time he scratched his belly as if he had fleas. Danny asked him where Brianna was, to which he curtly replied in a gruff voice, 'She's got more important things to do than chat to you.'

'I think I'll give breakfast a miss thank you,' Danny replied. He had the same thoughts about the old man making his food as he had had about the old lady the other night. While he had to admit the Irish stew turned out to be tasty enough, he wasn't prepared to risk this old guy making even a piece of toast!

Danny walked to the door, but as he did so something told him to take a look down the corridor where Brianna had disappeared. He turned to look and at the bottom of the passageway he could see her. She held her finger to her lips as if to signal to him not to say anything. She looked really nervous and then pointed upstairs. *Upstairs*, he thought. *How am I going to get up there?* He casually walked through the coffee shop door onto the pavement, glancing back to make sure that the old man (who was by this time stoking the fire in the grate) had not noticed him staring down the corridor.

When he got outside Danny casually crossed the road and looked up to the upstairs window of the shop. There he could see Brianna; she was holding a piece of paper and written on the paper were the words GO TO THE GATE TO THE CEMETERY AT TEN O'CLOCK TONIGHT. Danny put his thumb in the air to signal OK, he'd be there. Brianna just smiled back nervously and disappeared into the room.

The cemetery was right next to the walled area of the green field that led up to the mysterious wood which had intrigued Danny from the minute he'd got to Kilnurrah. It was at this wall that he'd met the little man who had so desperately wanted to tell him something, before his father had called and frightened him away. *What did that little man need to tell me that was so important – and why was he so frightened?* Danny wondered whether in some way or another he was connected to Brianna...

It was now eleven o'clock and Danny had to patiently wait until ten that night before he could maybe get some answers – and of course, he was looking forward to meeting Brianna in secret. He was excited at both possibilities. Of course, he was very concerned about his mother's broken leg, but he couldn't help but think how much easier it was for him now that all his family were two hours' drive away. He would never have been able to 'escape' at ten o'clock at night if they were there.

Danny went back to O'Grady's cottage and decided to get something to eat and maybe do some more reading to pass the time that afternoon and evening. He read for about an hour but found it too difficult to concentrate. There were so many things going on in his mind. He thought he'd do some fishing down at the river, as he'd noticed when he was in the grocer's that you could hire fishing rods there. He jumped off his bed and made his way out of the cottage and through the village to the grocer's. It seemed unusually quiet – not many people around that day. Anyway, he got the rods from the shop and made his way down to the river. He'd been fishing for about an hour when he heard some voices in the distance. There was a small forest behind him and he knew the voices must be coming from there.

He put his rod down and started to walk through the trees. The sun light was faintly coming through the trees and shone on the forest floor. Bluebells lined a path that had been worn through the forest and Danny could see faerie rings. Annie had taken the children for a forest walk once at home, and they'd passed some toadstools arranged in a ring and she had told them that was where the faeries had had a party the night before. Every time Danny saw something similar he thought of this story.

As he walked further into the forest the voices became clearer, but the flowers became fewer and Danny couldn't hear birds singing any longer.

Suddenly Danny noticed what looked like an old tree root, which had been hollowed out. He was very surprised to see the old lady from the coffee shop sitting in the tree root together with the man who had tried to serve him that morning and a few more creatures that looked very similar. It seemed like they were holding a meeting of some kind. He knelt down behind a rock and listened to their conversation.

He heard the old lady say, 'He came to the coffee shop with his family – I am certain he's the one who's been sent to take Brianna back to Varderlaun.'

'He won't get past me, I'll make sure of that,' said the old man.

The old lady then answered, 'We must watch his every move, and Brianna must be kept here and never returned to the faeries.'

Danny thought to himself, *What on earth are they talking about? I haven't been sent from anywhere! And where is Varderlaun?* But now he was certain that Brianna was linked to all this and that she certainly wasn't working in the shop because she wanted to. He now knew that what he'd seen in the coffee shop was meant to be a warning to him to keep away.

Very quietly, Danny got up from behind the rock and walked slowly and carefully through the forest back to the riverbank, making sure he wasn't heard by any of the creatures he'd just seen. He picked up his fishing rods and ran as fast as he could back to the cottage.

By this time it was nine thirty. It was dark outside and again as if by magic the gas lamps had been lit. Danny had a wash and changed his clothes and then closed the door of the cottage and quietly made his way down the road, which was completely deserted. He walked towards the cemetery wall.

When he got there, there was no sign of anyone. It was quite creepy because it was very dark; there was a distinct shortage of gas lamps down there. All Danny could hear was the hoot of an owl in the trees and the rustle of leaves as it flew from one branch to another. Luckily, there was a full moon that night and that cast some extra light on the scene, but it did, however, make the place even more creepy.

He started whispering, 'Brianna, Brianna, where are you?' No reply. Then suddenly in the same bush where he'd seen the anxious little man, there was another rustle of the leaves. Danny jumped back. It had been scary enough seeing this during the day but during the night – well, that was even scarier. He stood with his back against the wall and didn't even think of going to see what was in the bush, and then without warning the same strange, frightened little man appeared.

Danny took a deep breath and put his right hand on his heart to make sure it was still beating. The little man spoke. 'Don't be afraid, Danny, I'm not going to hurt you. Please listen to what I have to say.' Danny just stood rooted to the spot, unable to speak, but he nodded as if to say 'go on then'. The little man then began to tell him the most extraordinary tale Danny had ever heard in his life:

'My name is Osheen; I am the guardian of the entrance to Varderlaun, the Land of the Leprechauns and the Faeries. You see that wood over there?' Danny nodded. 'It's called the Faerie Wood. Underneath the wood through a secret passageway in the Magic Oak is the entrance to Varderlaun. I've been sent here to ask you for your help.'

Danny, looking completely shocked, replied, '*Me*? Why, what can I do?'

'We know that you have the gift,' Osheen replied.

'What gift?' said Danny.

'The gift of being able to see things that other humans cannot.'

Danny then remembered the conversation of the creatures he'd seen in the forest and things began to add up.

Osheen continued with this extraordinary tale. He told Danny that Brianna was the Princess of the Faeries and the Leprechauns and that she'd been captured by the goblins that inhabited Kilnurrah. They could transform themselves into what looked like humans during the daytime but during the night they would turn back into goblins and they got up to all sorts of evil deeds. They had captured Brianna when she was six years old because she had ventured too far into the green field and her curiosity had taken her as far as the red gate. Oonagh, the evil Queen of the goblins, had wanted a daughter and would do anything to keep Brianna prisoner in the realm of the goblins.

Danny was very confused at this point and said, 'But Brianna looks quite human – not faerie-like.'

'That's the spell that the goblins have put on her,' Osheen replied. 'They have changed her into human form and taken away her powers, but really she's a faerie and a very beautiful one. The King and Queen of the faeries have cried every day since she was taken and our world has become a very sad one. Varderlaun used to be a happy and prosperous place but now we are poor and unhappy. Every night the King and Queen listen to the pipes playing the saddest songs. If things continue in this way then our world will be destroyed and the evil in the world will overcome the good. You must help us Danny, please?'

'How can I help you?' Danny asked.

'You are staying at the O'Grady place aren't you?' Osheen replied.

'Yes,' replied Danny.

'There used to be an old well on the site where the house was built. This well had an underground passageway that had access to Varderlaun. After Brianna was captured this underground passageway was blocked by the goblins and none of us could get through it. The goblins' evil force-field surrounded the cottage and even if we had got as far as the cottage we couldn't have got out, and we would've been captured. But because you are human, the force-field cannot harm you. You can come and go as you want, and because Brianna will be in human form when you take her to the cottage it won't harm her either.

'We have no safe way of getting into the realm of the goblins now because they've put a spell on the green field and if one of us walks upon that green field we'll be swallowed up and transported to Oonagh's palace where we'll become one of her slaves.'

'Well, how did you get here then?' Danny asked.

'Because I am the guardian to the land of the leprechauns and the faeries I have three wishes that not even the goblins have power over. I have used two of them already; one the other day when I knew you were going to be at the cemetery and the second tonight – I only have one left. I wished that I could be protected by all the powers of good to keep me safe when I made my journey to the edge of the green field,' Osheen explained.

'Just tell me what I have to do and I will help you,' Danny said.

Osheen told Danny that he must search the cottage until he found the secret passageway. When he'd found this he had to take Brianna to the cottage and they must both travel through the passageway and deliver her safely to her mother and father, the King and Queen of the leprechauns and the faeries, and then once again good would prevail in the world and the evil ones would lose their powers.

'But that's easier said than done – I could probably find the secret entrance easier than I could get Brianna to the cottage. There's an old man there who won't allow her to speak to me. I saw him in the forest earlier today when I was fishing, and he was with the old woman,' Danny said.

'That's Lorcan, Oonagh's eldest son. He's a very wicked goblin and not easy to trick, but I'll give you the last of my three wishes and you must use it wisely, to help you get past Lorcan.'

Osheen and Danny sat talking for over an hour about the plan but eventually it was time for Osheen to leave.

'I have given you all the information you need: it is up to you now. All that remains to be done is for me to bestow my wish on you. This means that I'll never be able to come across the green field again safely and that means that this is the last chance for Brianna to be reunited with her family and for good to return to the world – please don't let us down, Danny, *please*.'

Osheen then began to chant a spell. He danced around the bush three times, hopping twice on one leg and twice on the other, and in a flash of light he disappeared.

Danny, stunned by what he'd just seen and heard, sat down on the wall to gather his thoughts and catch his breath. He certainly didn't feel any different since Osheen had bestowed him with the power of a special wish, but Danny knew he had to do what Osheen had asked him to. The next thing was to go the cottage and search for the secret entrance.

Danny walked back to O'Grady's Well and immediately lit a candle. This searching had to begin tonight – he couldn't leave it until the morning.

He searched in the kitchen, tapping away at the floor hoping to hear a hollow sound but nothing; he went into the bathroom, tapping away as if his life depended on it, but still nothing; then he went into the lounge and he noticed that the fireplace had been boarded up and a paraffin heater was up against the wall. He tapped the wall surrounding the fireplace and found that it was hollow. He went back into the kitchen and searched for something hard that he could hit the wall with. There was nothing so he just unscrewed a leg from one of the kitchen chairs and started knocking down the panelling that surrounded the fireplace. He hammered, pulled and tugged and eventually the panel came away. Behind the wooden panel was an inglenook fireplace exactly like the one in the coffee shop. Danny stood back, trying to find some clue, but in candlelight it was difficult. Then he noticed that underneath the hearth there was a metal ring on the floor. He got hold of the ring and tried to pull but it wouldn't move. He put the leg of the chair that he'd been using as a hammer through the ring to give him more to pull on. He pulled once; he pulled twice and then the third time – the trap door opened. There was a sudden rush of air, which shot past Danny's face and up through the chimney.

This was the entrance to the land of the leprechauns and faeries that Osheen had spoken of.

Danny looked down the well and it seemed deep, dark and damp. He didn't relish the idea of going down there, but he remembered Osheen and the tale he had told and he knew he'd have to do what he could to get Brianna back to her Kingdom.

The next part of the plan would be the difficult part – getting Brianna to the cottage.

It was the early hours of the morning by now, and Danny could see that the sun was beginning to rise and a faint flicker of sunlight was struggling to get through the window. With more light he could see the full extent of the destruction he'd caused to the wall that had previously surrounded the fireplace. *If my mother could see this now...* Danny thought. Oh, what a thought! The slap on the back of the shoulder that he'd got from his mother with the loaf of bread the other day, would seem like a tickle with a feather duster compared to what she'd do to him now, if she could see this mess!

Danny was feeling exhausted – a lot had happened during the night and he felt so tired he had to sleep.

He was awoken later in the morning by his mobile phone ringing. It was his father. 'Hi, how are you?' Danny asked.

'Good news, Danny, we're coming home tomorrow – we'll be really glad to see you. Have you been OK?' Tom replied.

Danny's stomach did a summersault – he replied, 'Oh yes, yes,' trying his best to hide the nervousness in his voice and also trying to muster up as much excitement as he could at the thought of them coming back *tomorrow!*

Tom told Danny that they'd be home late the following day – around six o'clock as his mother was going to be discharged from hospital but they'd have to wait for her to get her medication and so on, and then make the two-hour journey back to the cottage.

Tom continued: 'We've decided we're not going to look for the ancestors any more; we've had enough – well, your mother has. We'll just have a peaceful couple of weeks fishing, cycling and doing whatever you want, Dan, and just give your mother time to rest.'

'Oh great,' said Dan, in the most wimpy voice he'd ever used.

The rest of what his father said became a blur as Danny's mind was working at a hundred miles an hour to try to think how he could achieve all he had to do in just over twenty-four hours!

This was a mammoth task and some serious planning now had to commence...

CHAPTER FOUR

Danny put the mobile phone on his bedside table and sat up with a start. He knew he'd have to work fast. He put his head in his hands for a few seconds and then looked up and rushed to the bedroom. Staring out he saw the wood and realised that his plan had to start that very minute.

It was now breakfast time again so Danny had a quick wash and set off towards the coffee shop. He had to find a way to speak to Brianna. At least she knew that there was a plan to get her out of the goblins' clutches, as somehow the faeries had got a message to her, telling her to tell him to meet Osheen last night.

Danny opened the door of the coffee shop and to his horror he came face to face with Lorcan. Danny gulped and hoped that goblins couldn't see if someone's heart was beating so fast it was almost coming out of their chest. He went to the table where he normally sat and took a seat. Lorcan's eyes followed him all the time he was in the shop; it was as if he knew what Danny's plan was, and worse than that, Danny also knew that he knew. He would have to act as 'normal' as he could, but even Danny was now beginning to question what 'normal' was in this place.

Lorcan came over to the table and said, 'Can I get you anything?'

'Yes please,' Danny said. 'A piece of coffee and a cup of toast.' Then he realised what he'd just said and repeated, 'Um, a piece of toast and a cup of coffee please.'

Lorcan looked at him with the same piercing eyes as his mother had the first night Danny had seen her sitting at the fireplace. Lorcan turned his back and walked down the passageway to get the coffee and toast. Danny gulped once more and took a deep breath. He had to get his heart rate down to a reasonable rate and get control of himself.

Just as he had gained control of himself, Danny felt someone tap him on the shoulder. He jumped what felt like three feet off the chair. He looked around and it was Brianna. She had appeared from a stairway that Danny had not noticed before – behind the table he was sitting at. The stairway had been hidden behind a curtain, disguising it very well and blending it into the background.

Brianna whispered, 'I don't have much time, did you see Osheen last night?'

'Yes,' Danny whispered, 'we've got to work fast, there's no time to lose – my parents are coming back tomorrow evening and I've got to get you out of here, back to faerieland and do some nifty DIY before my mother gets back – any suggestions?'

Brianna smiled and said, 'Come to the coffee shop again at four o'clock this afternoon just before we close, and I'll leave with you then.'

'Oh great,' Danny retorted, and sarcastically added, 'that sounds like a good idea – really easy that is! What about the swamp beast' (referring to Lorcan) 'out the back?' Danny could hear footsteps coming back down the passageway.

Brianna said, 'You'll know what to do – think of your wish and use it wisely – I'll see you at four.' She then rushed off towards the curtain, leaving Danny's heart racing even faster than it had before.

Lorcan appeared, shuffled up to Danny's table and said, 'Here you are – anything else I can get you?'

Danny was just about to say 'Yes – lost!' but then he thought he had more important things on his mind and very little time to do them, so smart comments would have to wait.

Danny ate his breakfast and then went back to the cottage – it was midday by now and the first thing that greeted him as he walked through the door was the partly demolished fireplace. He thought again of his mother's reaction to such a scene and screwed his face up in anticipation of what she would do to him if she saw this.

The living room was much lighter now and he could see further down into the well. There was a ladder attached to the side of the well, but the only thing was he couldn't see the bottom it was too dark. He knew he needed to get a torch, so he made his way to the grocer's. He passed all the people he'd passed the other day and they stared at him in the same way as before. He wondered whether they could read minds and whether they knew what his plan was – worse still what would they do to him if they caught him trying to carry out the plan!

Danny tried not to make too much eye contact with anyone just in case. He noticed again the hats everybody wore. He knew that Oonagh was aware that he could see what other humans couldn't. He earnestly wished he hadn't seen the old lady in the coffee shop the first night they had arrived, then maybe all of this wouldn't be happening... Remembering Oonagh's horrible ears, Danny could now understand the headgear they all wore – they obviously all had the same physical attributes.

Danny got to the grocer's and surprise surprise, they were fresh out of torches. He felt like all his plans were falling apart and time was definitely not on his side. He ran back to the cottage and searched through his father's luggage; he usually packed the most stupid things just in case.

Tom was a typical 'just in case' kind of guy. Danny put it down to the fact that he had been married to his mother for so many years, he'd had to adopt the 'just in case' feeling because of his mother's many mood swings.

Danny frantically searched and soon found a torch in the pocket part of his father's case. *Good old Dad*, he said to himself. Then he went back downstairs and started to climb down the well. The further down he went the blacker it got and he became increasingly grateful that he had a torch.

After descending for about ten minutes, Danny came to the bottom and to his surprise the well floor was dry. There was only one way forward and he shone the torch down the passageway. He could see that there had been a blockage of some kind but it had been worn away and it was possible to crawl through the hole. On the other side of the hole the passageway looked clear and Danny could see a very dim light in the distance, which he assumed was the entrance to Varderlaun. The passageway had a very uneven floor and the walls were dripping with water. There was a very strong damp smell and everything was quiet except for the sound of trickling water in the distance.

Danny didn't want to waste any more time, so he made his way back up the passageway to the cottage. It was now three o'clock in the afternoon and he needed to get ready to go back to the coffee shop by four o'clock. He had another wash and put on some clean clothes. He left the cottage and walked down the road once again, very nervously heading towards the coffee shop. His stomach was turning over and over and his heart was racing as if he'd just run a marathon. The inside of his mouth was very dry and he thought if he'd tried to speak his lips would have stuck together.

He got to the door of the coffee shop and he could see that Lorcan was there, so he quickly moved to the side of the door so that he couldn't be seen. Danny stood with his back flat against the wall, looked up and thought to himself, *How am I going to do this?* Then, as if by magic, it came to him – he would have to use Osheen's last wish; he'd wish that both he and Brianna could be made invisible for the next half hour. That should be enough time for him to get into the coffee shop, find Brianna, and for them both to leave the shop and get back to the cottage.

Danny had never really wished for anything before so he didn't want to mess this up. He took a deep breath and said, 'I wish for Brianna and me to be made invisible for half an hour.' He stood rigid as a post for a minute. He closed his eyes tight and then opened them again and walked to the window where he'd checked his appearance upon visiting Brianna for the second time. This time he wasn't checking to see if he looked good – this time he was hoping he wouldn't see anything! He opened his eyes and lo and behold he couldn't see any reflection – he was invisible!

It was now ten to four and Danny had to get into the shop before it shut. He could see Lorcan coming towards the door; he opened it, stepped out onto the pavement and looked up and down the street as if he were checking something. Whilst he was surveying the area, Danny slid in behind him through the open door. Lorcan then came back into the shop. Danny was standing only a few yards from him at this point and was terrified that Lorcan would be able to see him. But as Danny stood rooted to the spot, Lorcan just walked straight past him and showed no sign of knowing there was anyone else there. Danny heaved a sigh of relief as he realised that Lorcan definitely could not see him, but to double check he made some pretty rude gestures (which he had wanted to make several times before) and there was no response – now he was sure Lorcan couldn't see him.

Danny hurriedly made his way to the curtain that covered the staircase. He ran up the stairs and could hear someone crying in one of the rooms. He followed the noise and opened the door of one of the rooms and there he could see Brianna sobbing.

'It's me, Danny,' he whispered.

Brianna looked around the room but couldn't see anyone. 'Where are you?' she asked.

Danny then remembered that he was invisible, and said, 'I've used Osheen's last wish and have made myself invisible – if you hold my hand you will become invisible as well and we can get out without Lorcan seeing us.'

Brianna dried her eyes and the sparkle came back to them. She had thought that Danny wouldn't be able to get past Lorcan and that her hopes of escape had gone, but now she shot off the bed and Danny said, 'I'll put my hand out to hold yours – now don't be frightened, as soon as I touch you you'll become invisible but we will be able to see one another.'

Sure enough, as soon as Brianna felt Danny's hand in hers she could see him. They made their way to the bedroom door and could hear Lorcan calling, 'Brianna, Brianna! Where are you?' Upon receiving no reply, he went into the bedroom and then he screamed, 'Mother, mother, Brianna has gone!'

Out of another room came Oonagh. She looked exactly like she had the night Danny saw her in the fireplace. 'Where is she? *Where is she?*' Oonagh screamed frantically. They both started running around the coffee shop shouting Brianna's name, but in the meantime Danny and Brianna were heading out of the shop and running like the wind up the street towards the cottage.

When they got to the cottage Brianna suddenly stopped. 'I can't go in there.'

'Yes you can, you are in human form so the goblin force-field cannot harm you,' Danny replied.

They ran towards the door and inside the cottage. Danny grabbed the torch and said, 'Follow me.' He showed Brianna the trap door and the entrance to the well. 'I'll go first,' he said, 'you come down after me.'

Danny shone the light and led the way down the shaft. They got to the bottom of the well and then they could hear a sound above them. Shining the torch up the shaft, to Danny's horror he saw goblins coming after them, and leading the way was Oonagh.

Danny shouted at Brianna, 'Run, *run!* The goblins have found us and they're coming for you!'

Brianna replied, in a voice full of panic, 'I knew they would know where to come, they know this is the only safe way out for me.'

'Never mind about that now,' Danny said, 'we need to cause distractions and try to slow them down.'

Danny started to hit the side of the passageway, hoping that this would cause a landslide behind them and block off the goblins' path. He shouted to Brianna, 'Run, Brianna, run as fast as you can. I'll try to block their path.'

Brianna started running as fast as she could down the passageway, and as if by magic the sides of the passageway lit up; at every step she took a light appeared at the side of the tunnel. Danny couldn't believe his eyes, but he didn't pay too much attention; he was more concerned with trying to stop the goblins, who were gaining on them.

Danny could now see the goblins; they were running like the wind and were such a frightening sight. They had all assumed their goblin form and all had huge blisters over their faces, which were weeping a smelly pus. They were making snorting noises and screaming like frightened pigs. The stench in the tunnel was becoming unbearable, the goblins' mouths were dripping with saliva from their rotten teeth.

To his horror Danny could now see the corkscrew-shaped ears being put to their full potential. Every time he managed to cause a blockage in the tunnel the goblins would use their ears like power-tools and they were boring holes in the blockages to remove them!

Meanwhile, Brianna was still running and in the distance she could see the lights of the world she had left so many years before. Then disaster struck; she turned to check where Danny was and he'd fallen and got his foot caught under some wood. She was within a few hundred yards of home and safety but Brianna turned around and started back down the tunnel towards Danny. Danny could see what was happening – one way he could see the goblins hurtling towards him and the other way Brianna was running back to help him, running into the path of the goblins. The perspiration was dripping from him, his clothes were torn and he was in pain. He couldn't move his foot, it was well and truly trapped, and then suddenly Brianna started to change from a beautiful girl into a beautiful faerie. She sprouted a pair of filigree wings, her hair shone like sunshine even though they were underground and was flying in the wind behind her as she flew to where Danny was trapped and landed by his side. Danny looked at her in amazement. She had totally transformed and was even more beautiful then she had been as a human. Her blue eyes shone like deep pools and her face shone as light seemed to radiate from it.

Danny shouted at her, 'Brianna, you've got to go, leave me I will be fine. Go, *go!*'

Brianna answered softly, 'No, my powers have returned now and I can help you.' She touched Danny's foot and it was immediately freed. She took him by the hand and they both flew down the passageway towards the distant light. Danny felt so strange; here he was holding the hand of a

faerie and flying through the air like it was the most natural thing to do! It was an effortless feeling, like some supernatural force was travelling through Brianna's hands.

The goblins were now being left far behind in the tunnel in the dark – each time Danny and Brianna passed through a section of the tunnel it returned to darkness. The magic of the tunnel was lighting the way for them to reach safety. Danny was amazed – this experience was unbelievable and yet he had to believe it, it was happening to him!

The noise of the goblins was getting more and more distant, and then, as Danny and Brianna hurtled down the tunnel, a most beautiful sight lay before them.

They had arrived in Varderlaun.

Danny couldn't believe his eyes. Standing at the entrance to Varderlaun was Osheen. He was jumping up and down from one foot to the other, clapping his hands with glee. His face had the biggest smile on it and he was shouting, 'Thank you, Danny Delaney, thank you from Varderlaun, the realm of the faeries and leprechauns!'

They had at last arrived at the River of Feardon; this was the entrance and this was where Brianna would be reunited with her mother and father, King Fearlan and Queen Donlana. Both Danny and Brianna got into the boat that Osheen had brought to the shore and they sat down and took a deep breath; they were home – well, at least Brianna was. Then they heard the goblins – they were almost at the riverbank when there came an almighty splash and a wooden box blocked the passageway completely, bringing with it several tons of earth. It would take even the goblins several hours to get through that lot, and by then Brianna would be safely home.

At first, it looked like just an ordinary wooden box, but then Danny shouted, '*Wait!*'

Osheen stopped rowing the boat. Danny noticed a plaque at the side of what he could now see was not an ordinary wooden box but a coffin. The plaque read:

Here lies Thomas Delaney, died 1775, who lived in Kilnurrah all his life. He saved all his money and never took a wife.

As they looked at the coffin, the lid opened and out fell thousands of gold coins and a very fragile skeleton. The landslides in the tunnel had made the ground below the cemetery unstable and good old great, great, great uncle – Danny's great, great, great grandpa's brother – had come to his rescue; not only that, but he'd also revealed his life savings, which had been buried with him!

Osheen, Brianna and Danny were dumbstruck – what a dilemma! There before Danny was treasure that had belonged to his ancestor and he couldn't go back for it.

Osheen said, 'Shall I go back for you and not save Brianna – it's your choice?'

'No, we must go on – keep on rowing, Osheen,' Danny replied.

Osheen smiled to himself and rowed the boat with all his might, and then they came to the banks of safety at last. It had been difficult for Osheen to give Danny the option to return but he had to test him. Danny took one more look at the coffin spilling gold pieces into the river, but his time he noticed that the river was no ordinary river; it was the most beautiful colour blue he'd ever seen, and all over the top of the water it seemed like diamonds were dancing on the ripples. When he turned around he saw Varderlaun – it was such a sight to behold. Hundreds of faeries and leprechauns ran to help Brianna off the boat and there, standing on the hill overlooking the river, were her mother and father, still crying, but this time the tears were of joy that their little girl had been returned to them.

Osheen, Brianna and Danny were escorted to the faerie palace which was covered in gold and there was a fine feast waiting for them. The goblets they drank from were encrusted with precious jewels and plates and knives and forks were made of pure gold and everyone was dressed in the finest silks. Danny thought to himself, *Hang on a minute Osheen said that they had become poor.*

Osheen must have been able to read his mind and said, 'Yes, that's right Danny, we were poor but look at my clothes now compared to when you first met me. When you brought Brianna back to our land you brought back more than just Brianna, you showed us that there is still some good in the world and the good things have returned to us again. You could have got off the boat and recovered your ancestor's treasure but you didn't; you stayed and you made sure that Brianna would get back safely. You put the safety of someone else before your own needs.'

King Fearlan and Queen Donlana approached Danny and the King said, 'Thank you, Danny, you have returned our daughter to us and have helped the good in the world to overcome evil and we will always be in your debt. Choose your gift – choose anything your heart desires and it shall be yours.'

Danny looked over at Brianna. She looked so beautiful and even though she had now completely transformed into a faerie and could never be truly happy in the human world, he could still remember what she looked like when she was a human. Although he'd only known her for a very short time she was very special to him.

Danny turned to the King and said, 'I just wish that one day I could meet someone as beautiful as your daughter and always be happy with her.' He walked towards Brianna and kissed her softly on the cheek. 'I must say goodbye now,' he said.

'I will show you the way out over the fields – it will be safe now,' Osheen replied.

Danny looked back and saw a human tear trickle down Brianna's face and then he turned his back and followed Osheen.

The path led up to the wood and to the edge of the field. At the entrance to the field Osheen said, 'Goodbye, my friend, and may you always be happy.'

Danny looked out over the field and he could see the cottage and his bedroom window in the distance. He turned around to say goodbye to Osheen but he'd disappeared. Danny shouted, 'Osheen, Osheen, where are you?' but there was no sign of Osheen, he had disappeared.

Danny started to walk across the field and when he got to the red gate he stopped and looked back. Where the wood had been dark and dismal looking, now the sun shone through the trees and the forest floor seemed to be sparkling. He smiled, opened the gate and walked towards the cottage.

Danny glanced at his watch; it was five o'clock. Where had all the time gone? What about the wall in the lounge? He ran up to the cottage and bolted through the door, looking anxiously towards the fireplace. To his amazement the wall was exactly as it had been when they arrived; there wasn't a speck of dust out of place. Danny gulped with relief. His mobile phone was ringing he dashed to answer it. It was Tom.

'Hi Dan, we're about fifteen minutes away from the cottage, we'll be with you shortly.'

'Oh that's good, I'll be glad to have some company,' Danny said, with a giggle in his voice.

Sure enough, about fifteen minutes later the car pulled up and they all got out. His mother had to be helped with her crutches but Ethan and Mary Ann ran to give Danny a hug at the door. Tom helped Annie as they walked to the door and as they approached Danny, Tom asked, 'Did you miss us?'

'I hope there's no washing up to do,' Annie said.

Danny just smiled – things were back to normal and once everyone was in the cottage and the door was closed, the door was closed temporarily on Danny's adventure. He knew there was no point in telling his family what had happened, but he knew deep down that he'd always have a link with this place and one day he would return...

CHAPTER FIVE

Many years later when Danny was twenty-five years old he started working for an archaeological company in Boston who specialised in excavations in Ireland. The pay was very good and they supplied Danny with his own apartment.

One day, just after he'd moved into his new apartment, a knock came at the door. Standing there was a colleague of Danny's, who said, 'I've come with some good news for you. We've been doing some excavation work in Kilnurrah in the west coast of Ireland and have found some items belonging to your ancestors. We've tried to locate your father but unfortunately we don't know his address so we've got a cheque to hand to you for $100,000.'

Danny's jaw just dropped open. After he'd composed himself he said, 'What kind of items did you find?'

'Some very old coins that were buried underneath your ancestor's coffin and they've been valued at $100,000, so since you are the only relative we can locate you get the cheque. We need someone with your knowledge of the area to go over there before we send the next team out to find out exactly what is needed. The men we sent to do the dig don't know enough about the area to find out more and they got homesick after a month! We need somebody reliable and who has some connections out there to help investigate – will you go, Danny?'

Danny immediately said yes. Just as his colleague was leaving Danny's apartment he turned around and said, 'Oh, just one more thing Danny; the men who came back from Ireland said they sensed something really strange about the area they were digging. Some had very strange glimpses of *little people* but we've put that down to the fact that maybe they had one drink too many.'

Danny laughed nervously and said, 'Oh, that part of the world can play tricks on you, you know, I wouldn't take too much notice of that.'

Danny of course knew what they had seen, but this meant that the 'little people' must have been trying to get help from someone for some reason. They would never have risked being seen otherwise…

Danny was of course delighted at the news about the coins buried with his ancestor. He tried to seem surprised, but of course he'd known they were there. It had been a pure coincidence that they'd started archaeological digs in that area. Danny thought back to the strange goings on that had happened almost ten years earlier and felt all this was happening for a purpose. He just knew that there was trouble out there and he had to go to investigate. Danny decided to set off to Kilnurrah as soon as he could.

Danny got himself ready and travelled to the airport for the next flight to Dublin. The plane journey brought back many memories of his first trip to the Emerald Isle and the adventures that he'd experienced there. He had always known that he would return and that the story was not over.

As the plane came in to land Danny heard the pilot say almost the same thing as the pilot said the first time they all landed there as a family, which set Danny to thinking about how his family looked now compared to how they were then.

Ten years had made a difference to them all in one way or another. Tom was still a handsome man but his hair had gone grey suddenly – practically overnight! Danny couldn't help but think all those years of being married to his mother had finally taken their toll.

Annie's weight had ballooned even more but her temper was not as bad – she had definitely mellowed with age. Danny was glad of this because it meant his mother and father had grown closer since the children had grown up. Ethan had gone to university and had lost his puppy fat, now he had become a babe magnet, as he liked to be called, and certainly did not have any shortage of female admirers. Mary Ann was no longer the plain Jane, she had grown into a very pretty teenager and now wore contact lenses having long since ditched the spectacles. She was very bright and was doing well in college and had plans to become a doctor.

Danny was reasonably happy with where he was in his life, but since leaving Ireland it was as if he'd left a part of himself there all those years ago. If he was really honest with himself, it was the only place where he really felt wanted and needed. He had had a reasonably happy childhood and his parents had been good parents, but he'd always known he was different in some way. It was not until his holiday in Ireland ten years earlier that he'd fully appreciated exactly what that meant.

Danny got off the plane and walked through the airport building to the same car hire stand as his father had done all those years before. As he walked passed the shops he smiled to himself when he saw the toy leprechauns. They really didn't look like Osheen, and Danny wished he could go into the shops and tell them what a *real* leprechaun looked like. But he thought the possibility of him being taken away by men in white coats would get in the way of the next quest that he may have to go on. It was easier to let the toy manufacturers believe what they wanted.

Eventually Danny arrived in Kilnurrah. He felt as though

he'd never left. He had a strange feeling inside as if this was where he should be – this was his real home. He had managed to make a hasty call to the local tourist board before he left and luckily O'Grady's Well was available. He made his way to the cottage and parked the car outside. He switched the car engine off and sat in the car just looking at the old house.

It now needed a coat of paint but all the emotions of the day he helped Brianna flooded back to him. It was as if it were yesterday. He turned his head and looked down the road that passed the coffee shop and feelings of excitement, apprehension and fear filled his mind, and then came the feelings of friendship that he felt for Osheen and then the overwhelming love that he had felt and still did feel for Brianna.

Danny got out of the car, got his cases from the boot and walked up the path to the front door of the cottage. As he walked in he remembered the holiday they had shared as a family as vividly as if it were yesterday.

It was as if the inside of the cottage had stood still in time; everything was as it was when they left after their holiday ten years earlier. Danny made his way upstairs and went to his old room; this also was exactly the same. He dropped his luggage in his bedroom and decided he didn't have any time to waste. He had to find out exactly what had happened and he had to find out soon.

After having a quick freshen up, Danny left the cottage and walked down the cobbled street towards the coffee shop. When he got nearer the first thing he noticed was that the sign no longer read 'OONAGH'S COFFEE COTTAGE'; it now read 'LORCAN'S' and just that. Danny had remembered what a man of few words Lorcan had been, so the brief title was understandable. Danny had grown designer stubble, so he felt sufficiently disguised to have a closer look through the window. There he saw Lorcan, who actually looked the same age and no older than he had looked ten years earlier. He was talking to a younger, strange looking man, who looked even more menacing than him. This younger man had dark, staring eyes and was taller than Lorcan and thin with unkempt hair and a straggly beard. He was walking around the shop in a stooping manner as if he were scrutinising everything he could see. Danny watched as Lorcan disappeared down the corridor.

Danny then took a deep breath, walked into the coffee shop and sat down. Even though his appearance had changed, walking back into the coffee shop brought back the same feelings inside: his heart was racing, his stomach was churning, and Danny had to try really hard to keep a grip on himself.

The younger man came over and said, 'What can I get you?'

'A coffee and a piece of the carrot cake please,' Danny answered. He'd noticed this over on the counter and it looked quite tasty – but he hoped he was not inheriting his mother's passion for sweets. He had noticed in the last few years that he was drawn to such things more than ever before. This was something he was going to have to watch!

The strange man shuffled over to the counter and brought him the cake and coffee. Danny heard Lorcan's voice shouting, 'Mallachi, Mallachi come here!'

The young man answered in a low, grunting voice, 'I'll be there just now, Father.'

It suddenly dawned on Danny that this was Lorcan's son and that each generation of goblin became more menacing than the last. Oonagh had been strange looking, Lorcan was disgusting and strange but Mallachi was disgusting, strange and even more menacing, even in his human form! Danny tried not to imagine how he might look when he assumed his goblin form. That was the kind of image that he didn't want in his head.

As he drank his coffee and ate his carrot cake, Danny watched Mallachi disappear down the corridor. His mind wandered back to all the things that had happened to him in that very shop. Everything seemed the same; the candle holders, the fireplace, the curtain hiding the stairway, even the sign which said PLEASE RING FOR SERVICE. It was as if the whole village had stood still in time, but where was Oonagh – why had the name been changed?

Then Danny's mind was drawn back to Brianna and he wondered how and where she was now – he hoped that she was still safe in Varderlaun. His feelings of apprehension now turned to feelings of fondness and he felt a warmth inside that he had not felt since he had last seen Brianna. Then an alarming thought entered his head – had she found a husband in Varderlaun? Danny had not had any particularly serious relationships. He'd had some girlfriends but somehow had never felt close enough to any of them to build a lasting relationship.

Danny got up from the table and left the payment for his food on the counter. He walked to the door and then he had the same urge as he'd had many years earlier – he looked back towards the fireplace. The fireplace was also the same but this time he didn't see Oonagh, this time the fire was dancing in the hearth and then suddenly he heard a voice from the fire echoing up into the chimney, saying, 'Leave this place Delaney, leave, leave...' and then a menacing laugh.

Danny quickly left the coffee shop and made his way back to the cottage and upstairs to his bedroom, where he sat at the bottom of the bed. He thought he recognised that voice but couldn't think who it was. He looked out of the window over at the faerie wood. He thought, *If only I could see Osheen – he'd tell me what was happening and why I've been brought back to Kilnurrah.*

It was now dusk in the little village. The lanterns at the side of the pavements had once again been lit by someone or something. Everything in the little village seemed so peaceful and quaint, but Danny knew that there was something wrong. He had a feeling inside like the calm before a storm...

Danny did not get much sleep that night, he tossed and turned, his mind trying to think of a way to get to talk to Osheen and also thinking about the voice from the fireplace. He eventually drifted off into the strangest dream. Osheen was standing by the fireplace in the cottage and pointing to the trap door which went down the well – Osheen was telling Danny that he needed to get to Varderlaun via the trap door.

Danny suddenly awoke – Osheen had got the message to him in his dream – he had to start work immediately.

CHAPTER SIX

Danny remembered that the tunnel to Varderlaun had become blocked when he'd taken Brianna back to her people, but he had no idea what state it would be in now after the workers had been excavating in the field above. It could have even caved in underneath all the weight of the excavation equipment. However, it was his only chance. The good thing was, this time he'd come prepared with equipment to dig with – not like before. He was convinced that if he could get through before, it would be easier this time.

Danny went downstairs and pulled the fireplace aside; the trap door was still there. He pulled the ring as he'd done before and thank goodness the passageway was clear. He started on his way down the well and got to the bottom. It smelled really damp and droplets of water could be heard dripping in the distance. He hurried down the tunnel as fast as he could in the direction of Varderlaun. He had come equipped with a torch this time as he thought he would not have the luxury of the tunnel just lighting up at each step as he had before. He switched the torch on but then disaster struck: the torch wouldn't work. He hit it on the side of the tunnel and there came a brief flicker of light but it dimmed even more. Danny heaved a heavy sigh. How was he going to get through the darkness of the tunnel without a light? Just as he thought all was doomed, lights started to shine as they had done all those years before on the walls of the tunnel. Danny now knew that Osheen was behind this and that he was expecting him.

Danny walked through the tunnel; with each step he took another light shone to guide him on his way. He smiled to himself and immediately feelings of excitement entered his heart – he was going to meet his old friend again, he knew that for certain.

The tunnel was remarkably clear and as he neared the River of Feardon, the lights shone on the water.

Eventually Danny came to the riverbank and he could see where his relative's coffin had been lifted away by the excavators, through a massive hole above him. This part of the tunnel ran underneath the graveyard, and the excavators had been digging close to the wall of the graveyard where Danny had met Osheen for the very first time. They had probably assumed that the river was just an underground river and hadn't paid much attention to it.

Danny got in the small boat that was at the waterside waiting for him and rowed across the river to Varderlaun.

As Danny rowed across the water, haunting Irish pipe music started playing, just like the music that he'd heard in the woods the first time he'd looked out of his room in Kilnurrah.

Eventually Danny got to the opposite riverbank and as soon as he stepped out of the boat hundreds of leprechauns and faeries ran to meet him, and running in front of them all was his old friend Osheen.

Danny felt overwhelmed and happy. He couldn't keep his emotions under control any longer and he could feel tears rolling down his face.

'Danny, Danny we are so glad to see you. Thank you for coming!' shouted Osheen.

Danny composed himself and said, 'What's been happening here?'

Osheen sat down on the side of the riverbank and put his head in his hands and started crying. He looked very tired and his clothes were in tatters. As Danny looked around at the other leprechauns and faeries he could see they all looked sad and very poor.

Danny sat down beside Osheen and put his arm around him and said, 'Take your time, Osheen. Don't get upset, my old friend, tell me all. I'm here now. I'm here to help and everything will be all right.'

Osheen dried his eyes with an old rag from his pocket and then started to tell Danny all that had gone on since he'd left.

When the coffin dropped, causing the blockage all those years ago, Oonagh had been trapped underneath the landslide and had been killed. After she'd died, Lorcan took over and ruled the world of the goblins and vowed revenge on Varderlaun and all its inhabitants for the death of his mother.

Danny told Osheen that he'd heard a voice telling him to leave Kilnurrah when he was in the coffee shop. Osheen said, 'That was probably Oonagh's ghost, she still haunts the village.'

Lorcan, together with his son, Mallachi, had managed to perpetrate more evil than anyone could imagine. They had been plotting their revenge on the faeries and the leprechauns for years and their ultimate plan was to take them from their peaceful land and make them all prisoners and slaves. The leprechauns and faeries had managed to keep them at bay for many years by using their powers and wealth but now they were growing very weak and had practically nothing left to defend themselves with. There was also the threat of the impending Goblin Eclipse, which would give the goblins ultimate power and make them unstoppable.

This Goblin Eclipse was due to occur on the night of the tenth day of the tenth month of the tenth year after Oonagh had died. When this Eclipse happened, Osheen explained, they would definitely take the faeries and leprechauns prisoner and their lives would be terrible, evil would take over the world completely. This Eclipse was due to take place in forty-eight hours' time.

Danny said, 'My boss told me that the men who were working here had gone home with stories of seeing little people.'

'Yes,' Osheen said, 'they were working in the field at the edge of the graveyard doing an archaeological dig when we helped them find your ancestor's gold. They saw the name on the coffin and made some enquiries and found that it belonged to your family. They then contacted your company and we knew you'd get a message somehow. We knew that you would come. We desperately need your help, Danny, we have to get to the Goblin Palace to get the Eye of Galleesh – their powerful weapon – before the Goblin Eclipse, but first we have to get past the dogs of the underworld.

'These dogs are called Mahdrig and Orhdrig. These are savage dogs with fangs like knives and claws which can rip you apart with one scratch. They are tied up by large chains and only Lorcan and Mallachi have the enormous power needed to control them. Even the other goblins are terrified of them. They are massive hounds, with matted coats and the stench around them is disgusting. Even if you could get past these dogs there is then a deep fiery pit of serpents which constantly spit out putrid smelling venom. If a spot of this venom touches you it means instant death.

'The goblins will be having a meeting at their sacred spot in the Forest of Grondan tonight in the hollowed-out tree, where you saw them many years ago, by the river. Go there and listen to what they have to say.'

'Don't worry, my friend, I've been sent here to help and that's exactly what I will do, no matter what it takes. I will go to the Forest of Grondan tonight,' Danny said.

'Before you go, Danny,' Osheen said, 'I have more dreadful things to tell you.'

Danny listened and Osheen told him something which was almost unbelievable.

This Goblin Eclipse was the most important thing in the whole history of the goblins. Many years ago Kilnurrah had been a bog and there had been a peaceful time when the goblins had lived in the bog and the leprechauns and faeries had lived a life of peace in Varderlaun. Unfortunately, Oonagh's ancestor, Gimlan, had become very greedy and wanted power over everyone. Gimlan had visited an evil sorcerer, Shadranach, who lived deep in the Forest of Grondan. Gimlan had asked for his help and promised Shadranach anything to get what he wanted. Shadranach then created Kilnurrah, the seemingly sleepy village where goblins could be in human form during the daylight hours but then have the powers to wreak havoc during the hours of darkness. The two evil ones hatched a plan that if the goblins lived in the sleepy village during the day, enticing humans into what looked like a tranquil setting, then they could do all the wickedness they wanted to the faeries and the leprechauns during the night but the most horrible thing would happen on the night of the Goblin Eclipse.

Shadranach's plan was to take over the human world, and he would do this from Kilnurrah on that night so both of the evil beings would benefit at that fateful time and evil would take over the whole world.

After hearing this Danny knew that this was more than saving the lives of the faeries and leprechauns he now had to save his world as well!

Danny said goodbye to Osheen, they hugged one another and he set off on his way to the Forest of Grondan.

That night there was a severe thunderstorm. Lightning lit the sky, dancing around the heavens like bony fingers stretching out to grasp the nearest thing and take it prisoner into the sky above, and the thunder sounded like some crazed being cracking a supernatural whip. It was as if everything in the universe was preparing for the fateful night which was less than forty-eight hours away.

Danny made his way through the Forest of Grondan. Even though he was now a grown man the atmosphere of the place still made him feel very uneasy. It was a cocktail of feelings that he felt he could well do without; fear, apprehension, the rush of adrenaline pulsing through his veins and the over-whelming urge that he had to help all who were depending on him.

It alarmed Danny that none of the world knew what was due to happen and it was even more frightening that it was all going to happen from what had seemed a sleepy little village. He simply had to help Osheen and his people and the rest of the human world as well.

As he came closer to the part of the Forest of Grondan where the old tree was, Danny could hear voices. He stopped still, the rain was beating down on him and there seemed to be a competition going on between the beating of the rain on the outside of his body and the beating of his heart on the inside. He started to walk very slowly in the direction of the voices. In front of him he saw Lorcan sitting in exactly the same place as Oonagh had years earlier.

Danny heard Lorcan telling the other goblins of Danny's time in Kilnurrah and the way he had rescued Brianna and taken her back to Varderlaun. He told them how it was the faeries, leprechauns and Danny's fault that his mother had been killed. Now it was time for vengeance on the people of Varderlaun and to fulfil the prophecy of Shadranach and Gimlan.

Lorcan instructed them all to get into their positions around the green field and in the passageway from the well to the River of Feardon. Their attack would take place the following night and at the moment of the Goblin's Eclipse they would hear the shrill howl of Mahdrig and Orhdrig – Lorcan's beloved hounds – and that would be their signal to launch the attack and take the faeries and leprechauns captive. Lorcan and Mallachi had positioned the goblins in the tunnel from O'Grady's Well, thus blocking this exit for the faeries and leprechauns so nobody could get through that way. There were also goblins stationed all over the green field so Varderlaun was totally surrounded. The only way anyone could get to or from Varderlaun would be by flying down from the mountain which overlooked the green field, on the back of the great bird – the Rionach. Lorcan started to cackle and all the other goblins joined in an evil, mocking laugh. They knew that no one could get up to the Rionach's nest; the cliff face was far too steep.

With the sound of the evil laughter ringing in his ears, Danny started to panic; there was no way that he could get back to Osheen, or get a message to him now. Or maybe there was – only one way; by getting to the Rionach.

CHAPTER SEVEN

Danny did not have any time to lose; he would have to go to the mountain now. It was almost midnight and the thunder storm was raging but he couldn't wait. He walked up the side of the mountain. The rain was beating down on him and making the climb very difficult. The mountainside was turning into mud and it was very slippery. Each step he took needed more effort. Eventually he stood at the bottom of the rock face and looked up with a determined expression; he was going to get up there – no matter what.

Although the rock face looked quite sheer there were tiny ledges that Danny was just able to grab on to, but the situation was made more dangerous by the very fact that it was so wet and the rock was slippery.

Up and up Danny went, climbing for what seemed like hours when eventually he arrived at the entrance of the Rionach's cave.

He started to walk towards the cave and heard the flapping of wings coming from inside. Deep inside the cave he could see a dim light so he followed the passageway that led him to this light. The rain was dripping off his head into his eyes and everything seemed blurry, he was guided only by the light. By this time Danny was completely fearless, he was driven by the overwhelming knowledge that so many were depending on him; there was no way he could let them down.

After walking for about ten minutes Danny could feel himself getting really exhausted and every step he took became harder. His feet felt like he was wearing boots made of cement and his legs were shaky. Deeper into the massive cave he went. He could see the stalactites and stalagmites hanging from the roof and growing up from the floor. Water was trickling down the side of the rocks. He then saw a slope in the path which seemed to lead downwards. He started walking down the very uneven tunnel floor until before him the cave lit up completely, and in front of him was the biggest bird he'd ever seen.

The Rionach looked like an extremely large eagle, its feathers were a golden colour and it had very bright blue eyes – not unlike Brianna's, but there was a sadness about them. When it saw Danny the Rionach looked startled and stood up and Danny guessed that it was about twenty feet tall.

'Who are you and what are you doing here?'

Danny told the bird what was about to happen and how he'd been sent to help the faeries and the leprechauns and all the humans in the world.

After listening intently to Danny, the Rionach said, 'You must rest now, my weary friend. I will take you to the Faerie Wood tomorrow, do not worry you are safe here; no one can harm you. You are a very brave man and your bravery will be rewarded.'

Danny immediately felt he could trust this creature, he seemed so kind. He curled up in the feathers of the Rionach's wing and fell into a deep sleep.

At daybreak the Rionach woke Danny. 'Danny we must go now, climb onto my back and grab hold of my feathers, you will not fall.'

Danny and the Rionach went back to the entrance of the cave and then with a massive flapping of its wings, the Rionach leapt into the air. Danny was holding on for his life. He knew that the Rionach had said that he would not fall off

but he wasn't so sure! They soared high above Kilnurrah. It was strange looking down on it from such a height, and then Danny could see the Faerie Wood in front of him. The Rionach flew down to a clearing in the middle of the wood.

'Here you are,' said the giant bird. 'I have done as I promised. All you need to do is believe in yourself and you will succeed in whatever you want to do.'

The Rionach spoke in such a wise way and its voice was so full of kindness. Danny asked, 'Why do you live alone in a cave away from everyone?'

The Rionach replied, 'I once lived amongst the goblins. My father was a goblin but my mother was a faerie. When the other goblins found out that I was not completely evil like them, they banished me for ever. I was transformed into a bird and left to live on the mountain and fend for myself. I am not welcome in either world, with neither the faeries and the leprechauns or the goblins, so I must live in the world between and only look down on the both worlds from my cave high above.'

'I'm so sorry,' Danny said. 'I wish I could help you in some way...'

'It is enough for me to be able to help you to help the faeries and leprechauns, there is too much evil in the world and the good needs to overcome it. If you need me again repeat this rhyme and I will come to help you, but I can come only once so use it wisely: "*Rionach great and mighty bird, please let my cry for help be heard*".'

The Rionach then flapped its great wings and soared up into the sky, returning to its lonely dwelling.

CHAPTER EIGHT

Danny ran to the opening in the Magic Oak in the Faerie Wood which led to Varderlaun and saw Osheen hurrying towards him. Danny told his friend what he'd heard in the forest and that there was very little time left as the Eclipse was due that night.

'There is only one thing that will save us; we must get into Lorcan's palace and get the Eye of Galleesh.'

Osheen explained to Danny that the Eye of Galleesh was the nerve centre of the goblin's world and it was where they got all their powers from. The Eye of Galleesh was a crystal ball, centuries old. It had an eye inside it and a powerful force-field surrounding it which protected the goblins.

Galleesh was Gimlan's brother, a Bogman (an ancestor of the goblins) and had lived centuries earlier and who had superhuman powers. He was also very wicked and ruled the underworld with a rod of fear. He was eventually overthrown and captured by Brianna's great, great grandfather. The faeries destroyed him but one part of him survived – his eye. The goblins found the eye and have used its powers ever since for evil.

Without this eye the goblins would be powerless. If the eye was brought back to Varderlaun then the leprechauns and faeries would destroy it completely and all the problems would be over and the world could become a peaceful, good place once again. But that only dealt with the goblins. There was also the problem of Shadranach the sorcerer who was still alive but no one knew where he was and he hadn't been seen since Gimlan's day.

Osheen continued. 'The way to the goblins' palace is down a secret passageway underneath Kilnurrah.'

'How do I get to it?' Danny asked.

'Our only hope is to go to the witch – the Boggoran, who lives on the edge of the Forest of Grondan. We don't very often speak of her as it is said she can be a dangerous creature, but if we take some faerie dust with us this may persuade her to help,' Osheen said. 'This is the last of the faerie dust and after this is gone then we will have nothing magical left to help us.'

Time was running out fast and Danny and Osheen needed to get to the Boggoran as soon as they could. Maybe she could tell them something about Shadranach as well.

Danny needed to think quickly, he needed to summon the Rionach to fly them both to the edge of the Forest of Grondan, so he chanted the rhyme that the Rionach had given him: 'Rionach great and mighty bird, please let my cry for help be heard!' Suddenly, as he looked up into the sky, both he and Osheen saw a pair of great wings flying towards them. It was such a dramatic sight, the storm was still raging and yet the gigantic bird seemed oblivious to it, flying with such majesty and power.

The Rionach settled on the ground near Danny and said, 'Tell me, what I can do to help you?'

Danny said, 'We need to get to the dwelling of the Boggoran at the edge of the Forest of Grondan. Can you please take us?'

'Get on my back and I will take you both,' the Rionach answered.

They flew over the green field, Danny and Osheen hanging onto one another and the bird until they approached the river, close to where Danny had gone fishing years earlier. The Rionach landed gracefully at the side of the river near the entrance to the Forest of Grondan and both Danny and Osheen climbed off.

'Thank you, mighty bird, we could not have done this without you. Please tell me if there is anything I can do to help you in some way,' Danny said.

The Rionach's eyes changed from looking sad and suddenly seemed as though they were smiling.

'Go fulfil your quest and that will be thanks enough for me. I will then be able to look down on a peaceful world filled with only goodness and know that I helped you destroy the evil.' With that, the bird flapped its wings and soared into the sky. Danny was sad to see the Rionach leave and stood mesmerised, watching it fly out of sight.

Danny then felt Osheen tug at his coat. 'We must go, Danny,' said Osheen.

'Oh, I'm sorry, Osheen, I just feel so sad for the Rionach.'

Danny and Osheen then ventured into the Forest of Grondan.

Osheen led Danny to the Boggoran's cottage, which was made of very large stones placed one on top of the other. Danny couldn't help but think how precarious the stones looked. There was a very large chimney with smoke billowing out of it and a light in one of the windows.

'She's probably boiling up one of her potions in her cauldron,' Osheen said.

'What's this old woman like, Osheen?' Danny asked.

Osheen just looked at Danny in a guilty kind of way.

Danny said, 'What's wrong, Osheen? You've brought us here, we aren't in any danger, are we?'

'Well no, we're not in any *real* danger but…'

'How did I know there was going to be a "but"?' Danny interrupted.

'The Boggoran is a direct descendant of Galleesh,' said Osheen.

'*What?* Why should she want to help us?'

'She was once the Queen of the goblins,' Osheen replied, 'but she was not as cruel as her great, great grandfather Galleesh, and had some kindness in her heart. The goblins saw this as a sign of weakness and made Oonagh (her cousin) the Queen. The Boggoran was banished to the edge of the forest and the goblins cast her out from their world. Since then she's lived a solitary life but she does have some magical spells and potions which she can use for good.'

Danny and Osheen walked up to the door of the cottage and Danny knocked on it three times. Nothing happened at first, but then they could both hear footsteps approaching the door. They heard the door handle creak and the door started to open very slowly. Before them they saw a very strange looking woman. She wore a cloak which dragged on the floor behind her and a hood over her head. Her face looked extremely old and wrinkled and her hands were distorted with huge lumps on her joints.

'Who is this you have with you, Osheen?' she asked.

'This is the only one who can save our land from the goblins, Boggoran. Please could you help us? You are not completely evil like the goblins and they have done you wrong, please help us,' pleaded Osheen.

The Boggoran looked at Danny and said, 'Both of you come inside.'

The inside of the cottage was remarkably welcoming. Danny had expected it to be menacing, cold and dark but it was lit with what seemed like hundreds of candles all around the room, there was a wonderful smell of lavender coming from a bunch of fresh lavender that had been picked and put in a vase on the table. The room was spotlessly clean and tidy and over in the corner there was a roaring log fire in the fireplace where a cauldron was bubbling away.

The Boggoran approached it and said, 'I've been making some soup, would you like some?' Danny looked at Osheen and Osheen looked at Danny. Osheen then stuttered and said, 'W-w-well that depends on what's in it.'

The Boggoran laughed, and pulled away her hood. Although her face seemed old, she had very kind eyes and said, 'My friends, please do not be afraid, these are harmless vegetables which grow in the forest. Everyone thinks because I look old and live here on my own that I use any powers I have for evil doing. I have no interest in doing bad but I do not get the opportunity to do any good because everyone is afraid to come here. I have been given a reputation as a result of what people *think* that I do and not what I *actually* do.'

Both Danny and Osheen immediately felt that they could trust the old woman and heaved a sigh of relief. They took a bowl of soup and while they were eating explained to the Boggoran what was due to happen that night. They asked her if she could help them, and promised her that if she would help them get the Eye of Galleesh then she could become one of the faeries and leprechauns and live amongst them. They could transform her by using the faerie dust and then she could live out her life in peace. At the same time, she could get rid of the goblins that had done her such wrong many years earlier.

The Boggoran thought for a while and then finally she said, 'I will agree to help you get the eye.'

Osheen and Danny heaved a sigh of relief and sat while the Boggoran told them how to get to the Eye of Galleesh.

'I can give you three items that will help you get past the hounds and then the snakes, but the final one will be the most powerful. It will help you get past Lorcan and Mallachi. These two will be guarding the eye with their lives until the

Goblin Eclipse; they know this is the only thing that can enable them to carry out their plan.'

'The first item is a magic piece of meat. You must throw this to the hounds when you get near them. As soon as they smell the meat they will fall into a deep sleep and will not awaken until I command them to. The second item is a bottle which contains a magic flame. When you get to the pit, open the bottle. The flame will escape from the bottle and surround the pit of snakes as you pass, stopping them and their venom from getting to you. The third item is the most powerful but it must involve some skill on your part. It is the ancient rope which belonged to Galleesh himself. He used this rope to catch and bind many of those beings whom he took prisoner. The rope has its own magic but you must be accurate in the way you throw it. It must be directed precisely at those you wish to capture. You only get one attempt and if this does not work then the rope will disappear.'

Danny looked at Osheen and Osheen looked at Danny; neither of them had any experience of 'lassoing' anything, but they both knew they'd have to take the chance.

'One more thing, Boggoran,' said Danny, 'do you know where Shadranach is? We know of the pact made many centuries ago between him and Gimlan but want to make sure that he can't fulfil his side of the pact and take over the whole world.'

The Boggoran looked very frightened and replied, 'I don't know where Shadranach is, but I learned from my goblin father of the pact and it has always been a fear of mine that this day would come.'

Danny said, 'Well, what can we do? We must save both worlds.'

'I will come with you to the Goblin palace – if Shadranach is still alive then that is where he will be waiting for the hour when his pact will be fulfilled with the goblins. Leave him to me,' the Boggoran said. 'We have no time to lose, follow me.'

They packed up the items that the Boggoran had given them and the three of them left her cottage and went to the secret entrance to the goblin palace through the hollowed-out log in the forest. They travelled down a smelly, dirty passageway which was lit only by the torch Danny was carrying. The sides of the passageway were damp and the floor was very uneven and slippery.

As they got closer to the palace they could hear the growling of the hounds, Mahdrig and Orhdrig. Both Danny and Osheen were terrified. 'Don't be afraid, just do as I told you,' the Boggoran said. The hounds looked (and smelled) exactly like they'd been described.

Danny got the piece of meat from the bag around his waist holding all the items and threw it down before the hounds. Sure enough, as the Boggoran had said, they immediately fell asleep and Osheen and Danny very slowly walked past them.

The three of them walked on through the tunnel until they came to the pit of snakes. Danny took the bottle of fire from his bag and opened the top; immediately a fierce flame came from the bottle and surrounded the pit. The snakes were spitting and slithering about like mad things but the fire was protecting Osheen, Danny and the Boggoran as they ran past.

A few hundred yards down the passageway the stench was getting worse – it really smelt of goblin now. Osheen said, 'We must be very close to the palace, get the rope ready.'

They walked further on and there, before them, they saw the palace. It was an awesome looking place; dark, miserable and putrid smelling. There was a light in one of the windows. They approached the window and looked in. They could see the Eye of Galleesh on a throne with a pulsating light glowing around it. Next to it were Lorcan and Mallachi and, as they had feared, the old sorcerer too. They were speaking to the eye, worshipping it on their knees, asking for its powers to help them at the hour of the Goblin Eclipse, which was now only one hour away.

Osheen and Danny knew there was no more time to spare; they had to burst in and capture them now. They took one last look at one another and armed with the rope they were about to burst through the door of the palace when the Boggoran grabbed Danny by the arm.

'You cannot go in yet. You must let me deal with the sorcerer in the only way I know how.'

'What can we do to help you?' Danny asked.

'You cannot do anything, this is something I must do myself.'

Danny looked at Osheen in a very worried way, but Osheen just held the Boggoran's hand and kissed it.

'What are you going to do?' Danny asked.

The Boggoran did not reply but just smiled, turned her back on them and walked up to the door of the palace.

Danny was really worried. 'What's she going to do? Is she in any danger?'

'Danny, there is nothing you can do to help the Boggoran. Before she left her cottage I saw her getting a magic wand from behind her fireplace. I had heard of this wand but I'd never seen it before. The wand is called the Wand of Magellach – an ancient wizard who lived with the faeries until he was killed by Gimlan. The Boggoran must have inherited the wand from her mother because she was a faerie. The wand is the ultimate weapon that can defend good in all the world, but the person that uses it must sacrifice their own life when they destroy evil.'

'No! She mustn't do this, she's helped us – we can't let any harm come to her!' Danny exclaimed.

'It is her decision, she knew this before she left the cottage,' replied Osheen.

Danny started to run after the Boggoran but Osheen stopped him. 'Stop, Danny! The worlds, both ours and yours, will be destroyed tonight if she doesn't do this.'

Danny stopped and put his head in his hands. It was so unfair that this was going to happen, and he wasn't prepared to let the Boggoran go in there alone.

Seeing the Boggoran go into the room where the goblins and the sorcerer were, Danny immediately started to follow her, with Osheen following him. When the goblins saw the Boggoran they rushed towards her but from under her cloak she brought out the wand that was shining bright and ran away from the goblins towards the sorcerer. With one swing of the mighty wand she pointed it at him and he vanished into thin air.

Danny and Osheen burst into the room and headed toward the goblins, who were now fast approaching the Boggoran and the wand.

Lorcan and Mallachi pulled out the biggest swords Danny had ever seen from sheaths hanging from their belts. Osheen screamed at Danny, 'Now Danny, you must throw the rope now!'

Danny stared at the two goblins, took a gulp of air and threw the rope directly at them. Both Danny and Osheen held their breath – it was now the time to either capture the goblins or the rope would disappear in front of them and so would they.

As Lorcan and Mallachi lunged towards Danny and Osheen the rope wrapped itself around them. They dropped their knives, screamed and tried to break free but the more they struggled the tighter the rope got. It was now tightly wound around them and there was no way they could escape.

Without pausing for breath, Danny ran to get the eye from the throne. He grabbed it then both he and Osheen ran as fast as they could back towards the door. On their way they saw the Boggoran lying on the floor motionless. Danny pulled back the hood of her cloak and to his amazement she had been transformed into a beautiful young woman. The gnarled hands that had held the wand were now young and youthful and she had grown two filigree wings on her back. Danny held the Boggoran's head in his hands and said, 'Boggoran, Boggoran please say something!'

The Boggoran opened her eyes and whispered, 'Go, Danny, save your world and the world of Varderlaun and take Brianna to be your wife and live a very happy life.' With that her eyes shut and she was dead.

Osheen shouted to Danny that they must leave.

Everything the witch had said had worked but both Danny and Osheen were so sad that she had had to sacrifice her life.

The goblins positioned all around Varderlaun ready to take the faeries and leprechauns prisoner had no powers, but Danny and Osheen would still have to get the eye back to Varderlaun before the Goblin Eclipse.

They ran past the goblins in the field, who tried with all their might to stop them but to no avail as their powers had disappeared. Then eventually they got to the Faerie Wood and ran down the passageway from the Magic Oak to Varderlaun. King Fearlan and Queen Donlana were waiting for them. Osheen took the eye to King Fearlan and laid it on the table. King Fearlan then picked up a jar which was covered in sparkling rubies and emeralds and walked closer to the table. He opened the jar very carefully, put his hand inside and took out a handful of what looked like sand. He threw the sand at the eye and as it covered the eye it changed into faerie dust. As soon as the eye was covered in faerie dust it disappeared into thin air. Every faerie and leprechaun in Varderlaun let out a mighty sigh – it was done, the eye was gone, they were now safe for ever.

King Fearlan walked over to Danny, who was by now completely exhausted. 'My dear Danny,' he said, 'you have helped us once more. How can ever we repay you?'

'I need no repayment but I would like to see Brianna,' Danny said.

'She is here,' King Fearlan said. 'She has not smiled since the day you left.'

From an adjoining room Brianna appeared. She was a vision of loveliness. Her yellow hair was shining like the sunshine, and her bright blue eyes glistened as she smiled a smile which lit up the whole of Varderlaun. She was wearing a long silver dress with small sparkling diamonds all over it. As Danny walked towards her he noticed her eyes were filled with tears of joy.

'I've missed you and I've decided I'm never leaving you again,' Danny said.

They held hands and kissed before walking towards their new life together in the palace of Varderlaun.

So, my friends, this is the happy ending, but it is not the end of Danny's adventures. He will be asked to aid some other poor souls who need his help, and he will meet some new exciting creatures and have help from some old ones, but that is another story…

Printed in the United Kingdom
by Lightning Source UK Ltd.
108664UKS00001B/136-312